THIS WALKER BOOK BELONGS TO:

_____

_____

_____

For the Goodfellows

First published 2001 by Walker Books Ltd
87 Vauxhall Walk, London SE11 5HJ

This edition published 2002

8 10 9 7

This book has been typeset in Galahad

Printed in China

British Library Cataloguing in Publication Data:
a catalogue record for this book is
available from the British Library

ISBN 0-7445-8920-7

www.walkerbooks.co.uk

Little Baa

Kim Lewis

WALKER BOOKS

AND SUBSIDIARIES

LONDON • BOSTON • SYDNEY • AUCKLAND

Little Baa frisked in the field.
His Ma ate quietly beside him.

Spring and bounce and skip went Baa,
running through the grass with his friends.

Little Baa ran along the fence,
hopping over rocks.
Spring and bounce and skip
went Baa.

Soon he left his friends behind.

Then Little Baa
grew tired. He found
a hollow near some
trees and settled
down for a nap.

Ma ate grass until little by little
she was far along the field.

When Ma finished eating, she looked around. "Where's my Little Baa?" she said.

She couldn't see his spotty ears.

She couldn't smell his familiar smell.

She couldn't hear his little baa.

"Baa!" she called. "Where's my Little Baa?"

"Maa!" called lots of little lambs.
They came towards her, one by one.

"You're not mine," sniffed Ma to each.

None of them were her very own
the way Little Baa was hers.

The little lambs ran to their mothers.
Ma sniffed among the ewes.

"Have you got my Little Baa?" asked Ma.

"Go away," said the ewes, and stamped their feet.
"These lambs are ours, not yours."

Ma trotted sadly on.

The sun was starting to go down.

Ma's voice became a lonely sound.

She couldn't rest or eat or think.

"Baa!" she cried. "Please answer me!"

But there was only silence in the field.

Then the shepherd came with his collie, Floss.
He heard Ma calling and saw she was alone.
"Where's your little lamb?" he said to Ma
and strode off through the grass.

Little Baa woke up feeling cold and hungry.
He stretched and blinked and then he saw
the beady eyes of a border collie.

Floss didn't have Ma's spotty ears.
Floss didn't have his mother's smell.
Worst of all, Floss went "Bark!"
"You're not my Ma!" said Little Baa.

"Ma!" cried Little Baa, running every which way.

"Maa!" cried Little Baa, running round in circles.

"Wait, Floss," said the shepherd softly.

From far across the field,

Ma picked out the little sound.

It was the sound she wanted most of all

in the whole wide new spring world.

First Ma walked. Then she trotted.
Soon she was running fast.
"Baa!" she called. "Baa, Baa, Baaa!"

Little Baa ran to Ma.
He ran and ran and ran.
"Ma!" he said. "Ma, Maa, Maaa!"

Ma sniffed Little Baa all over, baaing gently.

"Where were you, Ma?" asked Little Baa.

"Looking everywhere for you," she said.

Ma stood quietly while he fed
because Little Baa was oh so hungry.
Then Little Baa snuggled down with Ma.

"Ma?" said Little Baa sleepily.
"Are you still there?"
"I am, Little Baa, I'm here," said Ma,
lying quietly beside him.

WALKER BOOKS BY KIM LEWIS